THIRTY-THREE
Multicultural
TALES TO TELL

Critical Acclaim for
Thirty-Three Multicultural Tales to Tell

"Easy-to-learn versions enlivened with unforced humor and clear, fluent language; most would take ten minutes or less to tell. Their readers will bring away a stronger impression of human culture's unity than its diversity."

—KIRKUS REVIEWS

"Pleasant DeSpain is the master storyteller who put this volume together, and we should thank him."

—TEACHING PREK-8

"A wonderful way to share the heritage of others. It is a wise choice for any school, public or home library and can be enjoyed by all members of a family."

—THE TAMPA TRIBUNE-TIMES

THIRTY-THREE
Multicultural
TALES TO TELL

By Pleasant DeSpain
Storyteller

Illustrated by
Joe Shlichta

A MERRILL COURT PRESS BOOK

PUBLISHED BY

August House Publishers, Inc.
L I T T L E   R O C K

Published 1993 by August House, Inc.,
P.O. Box 3223, Little Rock, Arkansas 72203,
501-372-5450.

Printed in the United States of America

10 9 8 7 6 5 4 3 2

LIBRARY OF CONGRESS CATALOGING-IN-PUBLICATION DATA

DeSpain, Pleasant.
Thirty-three multicultural tales to tell /
by Pleasant DeSpain, storyteller : illustrated by Joe Shlichta.
p.   cm.
Summary: A collection of folktales from around the world, selected for their "tellability."
ISBN 0-87483-265-9 (HB) : $25.00. —
ISBN 0-87483-266-7 (TPB) : $15.00
1. Tales. [1. Folklore.] I. Shlichta, Joe, ill. II. Title. III. Title: 33 multicultural tales to tell.
PZ8.1.D47Th   1993
398.2—dc20   93-1824

Executive editor: Liz Parkhurst
Illustrator: Joe Shlichta
Typography: Heritage Publishing Co.

This book is printed on archival-quality paper that meets the
guidelines for performance and durability of the Committee on
Production Guidelines for Book Longevity of the
Council on Library Resources.

AUGUST HOUSE, INC.   PUBLISHERS   LITTLE ROCK

For Gary, Lori, and Rob
My brother, sister, and nephew
Let's dance!

Acknowledgments

To my friends and colleagues who helped so much ...
I couldn't have done it without you!

Editor: Leslie Gillian Abel
Illustrator: Joe Shlichta
Story Ambassador: Peder Jones
Folklore Consultant: Margaret Read MacDonald, Ph.D.
Publishing Consultant: Doug DuBosque
Software Consultant: Daniel Higgins
Software Consultant: W. Bruce Smith
Family Consultants: Mark, Alma, and Kenny Langley

"The folktale is the primer
of the picture-language
of the soul."

—Joseph Campbell

"It does not require many words
to speak the truth."

—Chief Joseph, Nez Perce

CONTENTS

INTRODUCTION

LONG AGO, when I first began telling stories for a living, I fell in love with the purity and simplicity of the traditional tale. With this, my third collection of multicultural tales to tell, I'm convinced that we, the inhabitants of planet Earth, are *all* storytellers. The story we tell, with its infinite variations, is about being born, living life, knowing sorrow, knowing joy, dying, and again, being born. It's the story of human evolution.

I marvel at the fragile yet unbroken force that holds each and every life (story) as one and the same. Some say it is the stories we tell. I say it is the breath we breathe. Stories are told with words. Words are breath put into form. Perhaps the most common life experience shared by all is that we inhale and exhale. This is where stories truly begin and end.

As for these particular tales, they were selected on the basis of their "tellability," universality, and cultural integrity. They are simply told, as is my style, and contain within them room for your experience, expression, and style. I've attempted to balance the book with a fair number of tales from each of the major continents, and have included intelligent and strong boy/girl, woman/man, and animal/human tales. They are intended for both beginning and professional educators, parents (bedtime story experts!), and storytellers. And since I use "real" words, the stories will grow with the children who hear or read them. Hopefully, they will never grow out of them.

I recently received a call from a woman of age who had heard me tell the Russian tale, "Granddaughter's Sled" (page 91). She wanted a copy for a friend. "You're the storyteller who knows which words to leave out," she said. It was a profound comment.

Enjoy reading, learning, and sharing these tales, and may you, too, know which words to leave out!

OLD JOE & THE CARPENTER

A Tale From the United States

OLD JOE LIVED way out in the countryside all by himself. His best friend was also his closest neighbor. It seemed that they had grown old together. Now that their spouses had passed on, and their children were raised and living lives of their own, all they had left were their farms ... and each other.

But for the first time in their long friendship, they'd had a serious disagreement. It was a silly argument over a stray calf that neither one of them really needed. The calf was found on the neighbor's land and he claimed it as his own. Old Joe said, "No, no, now that calf has the same markings as one of my cows, and I say it belongs to me!"

They were stubborn men, and neither would give in. Rather than hit each other, they just stopped talking and stomped off to their respective doors and slammed them shut! Two weeks went by without a word between them. Old Joe was feeling poorly.

Come Saturday morning, Old Joe heard a knock on his front door. He wasn't expecting anyone and was surprised to find a young man who called himself a "traveling carpenter" standing on his porch. He had a wooden toolbox at his feet, and there was kindness in his eyes.

"I'm looking for work," he explained. "I'm good with my hands, and if you have a project or two, I'd like to help you out."

Old Joe replied, "Yes, as a matter of fact, I do have a job for you. See that house way over yonder? That's my neighbor's house. You see that creek running along our property line? That creek wasn't there last week. He did that to spite me! He hitched a plow to his tractor and dug that creek-bed from the upper pond right down the property line. Then he flooded it! Now we got this creek to separate us. I'm so darn mad at him! I've got lumber in my barn, boards, posts, everything you'll need to build me a fence—a tall fence—all along that creek. Then I won't have to see his place no more. That'll teach him!"

The carpenter smiled and said, "I'll do a good job for you, Joe."

The old man had to go to town for supplies, so he hitched up his wagon and left for the day. The young carpenter carried the lumber from barn to creekside, and started to work. He worked hard and he worked fast. He measured, sawed, and nailed those boards into place all day long without stopping for lunch. With the setting of the sun, he started to put his tools away. He had finished his project.

Old Joe pulled up, his wagon filled with supplies. When he saw what the carpenter had built, he couldn't speak. It wasn't a fence. Instead, a beautiful footbridge, with handrails and all, reached from one side of the creek to the other.

Just then, Old Joe's neighbor crossed the bridge, his hand stuck out, and said, "I'm right sorry about our misunderstanding, Joe. The calf is yours. I just want us to go on being good friends."

"You keep the calf," said Old Joe. "I want us to be friends, too. The bridge was this young fellow's idea. And I'm glad he did it."

The carpenter hoisted his toolbox onto his shoulder and started to leave.

"Wait!" said Joe. "You're a good man. My neighbor and I can keep you busy for weeks."

The carpenter smiled and said, "I'd like to stay, Joe, but I can't. I have more bridges to build."

And he walked on down the road, whistling a happy tune as he went.

THE TUG OF WAR

A Tale From Africa

ONCE LONG AGO Tortoise was crawling along a jungle trail. He had just been chased out of the river by Hippo and was not in a friendly mood. Suddenly, Elephant rushed across the path and nearly stepped on Tortoise.

"Watch where you're going, you big, lumbering fool!" cried Tortoise.

Elephant did not like to be insulted and replied, "You watch where you're going, tiny Tortoise, and also watch your sharp tongue. It could get you into trouble."

"You don't frighten me," said Tortoise defiantly. "I'm stronger than you realize. In fact, I'm as strong as you."

"No, you're not!" trumpeted Elephant. "You are too small to have my strength, and if you don't apologize for your silly boasts, I'm going to step on you!"

"I have a better idea," said Tortoise, as he took hold of a stout vine. "I challenge you to a contest of strength, a tug-of-war. You hold one end of this long vine with your trunk and I'll go down to the river with the other end. I will try to pull you into the water and you will try to pull me into the jungle. When I yell, 'Pull, O mighty beast, pull!' the contest begins."

"Very well," agreed Elephant, "it will be fun to make a fool of you."

Tortoise took the other end of the vine and disappeared into the thick jungle growth. When he arrived at the river's edge, he called, "Hippo! Hippo! Stick your head out of the water if you're brave enough!"

The huge hippo slowly surfaced and swam over to Tortoise. "Are you calling me, little one?"

"Yes, big one," answered Tortoise. "You chased me out of the river

earlier today, and now I'm mad. You think that you're strong because of your size. I'm going to show you that I, too, am strong."

Hippo was amused by Tortoise's angry speech and said, "Your words are bigger than your shell, little friend. How can you prove such a boast?"

"By challenging you to a tug of war!" said Tortoise. "You take this end of the vine in your mouth and I'll go into the jungle and take up the other end. You try to pull me into the river, and I'll try to pull you out of it. I'll yell, 'Pull, O mighty beast, pull!' when I'm ready."

Hippo laughed and said, "I agree. It will be fun to teach you some manners."

Hippo bit on the end of the vine and Tortoise walked back into the trees. Then he yelled in his loudest voice, "Pull, O mighty beast, pull!"

Both Elephant and Hippo began to pull, and they pulled and pulled with all of their strength, but neither could gain on the other.

"Tortoise is as strong as Hippo!" thought Elephant as he grunted and pulled even harder.

"Tortoise is as strong as Elephant!" thought Hippo as he strained and pulled harder still.

When he could see that Elephant and Hippo were growing very tired, Tortoise yelled, "Stop, stop! Let's call it a tie. I'm afraid that the vine will break!"

Both of the large beasts were happy to stop pulling.

Tortoise ran to Elephant, and as soon as Elephant caught his breath, he said, "You *are* strong, friend Tortoise, and I will be careful of where I step from now on."

Then Tortoise went down to the river and Hippo said, "I'm sorry for chasing you out of the water, little friend. You are much too strong to be joked with."

Tortoise was treated with great respect from that time forth.

THE LISTENING CAP

A Tale From Japan

⊙HERE ONCE LIVED a poor woman who faithfully visited the shrine of her guardian spirit each morning. She was so devoted that one day the guardian spirit left a gift for her in the shape of a small green cap.

She put the cap on, and to her great surprise, was able to understand what the birds, animals, and plants of the forest were saying. "It's a listening cap!" she cried happily.

Just then two robins landed on a nearby branch and began to converse:

"It's so sad about the maple tree," said one.

"How true," replied the other. "I heard it crying again last night. Do you know the story behind the tree's sadness?"

"Yes," said the first robin. "I was there the day it happened. The town mayor chopped down the maple in order to make room for a teahouse in his garden. Unfortunately, he didn't dig up the roots, and that's why the tree still cries out in pain. It isn't dead, nor is it alive. It just remains under the teahouse."

"Is that why the mayor is so weak and sickly?" asked the other bird.

"Yes," said the first. "The maple has put a dark spell on him. On the day the tree finally dies, the mayor, too, will be carried to his grave."

Upon hearing all of this, the poor woman rushed home and made herself up to look like a wandering doctor. With the listening cap still on her head, she walked up to the door of the mayor's grand house. The wife of the mayor gladly welcomed the doctor. She asked her to examine her husband, adding that she had already tried all the known remedies without success.

"When did your husband have the teahouse built in the garden?" asked the doctor.

19

"Just last year," said the mayor's wife.

"And has your husband been sick ever since?"

"Yes," she said. "How did you know?"

"It's a special talent of mine," answered the doctor. "Before I examine your husband, I would like to have a cup of tea in the garden."

"Of course," she replied. "I'll fill the pot."

The phony doctor went into the teahouse and sat quietly. Soon she heard a low moan coming from beneath the floor.

"Is that you, poor maple tree?" asked a butterfly floating into the room. "Are you feeling any better today?"

"No ... I feel much worse ... in fact, I'm going to die soon, and when I do, so will the mayor. I'll see to that."

"Please don't die," said the butterfly.

"No, don't die ... don't die...." echoed the garden roses.

The doctor rushed to the mayor's bedside and said, "If you want to live, have the teahouse torn down at once! Then tend to the maple whose roots still rest beneath it. Help the tree to grow strong again."

He agreed and told his servants to demolish the teahouse. The sickly mayor cared for the maple himself. Soon it began to send healthy green shoots into the air.

"I will live!" cried the tree at last.

"The maple lives!" shouted the garden.

Within a few days the mayor was feeling much better, and after only two weeks, he was well and strong again.

The wandering doctor was given a large bag of gold, and with the listening cap still on her head, the once poor woman went on her way with a gentle smile upon her lips.

RABBIT'S LAST RACE

A Tale From Mexico

SINCE LONG AGO, Rabbit has been known to be a fast runner, even though he once lost a famous race to Tortoise. However, that was a very long time ago.

Rabbit liked to brag about his swift speed and that is why Frog, growing tired of such boasting, challenged him to a new race.

Rabbit accepted and wanted to race that very afternoon. Frog said, "It is my nature to swim through the water, not run across the ground. I'll need three days to practice running."

(I'm sure that you have played leapfrog before, and know that a frog doesn't actually run at all. Instead, he leaps or springs from one place to the next.)

Rabbit was so confident of winning that he let Frog choose the race course. Frog decided it would be the most fun to race through the tall swamp grass from the bottom of the hill all the way down to the river.

During the next three days clever Frog called together all the frogs that lived on the river who were the same size as himself. That was nearly four hundred frogs! He had them line up in the tall grass, about one good leap apart, from the hill to the river. Then Frog hopped up to Rabbit and told him that he was ready to begin the race.

"Good," said Rabbit. "Now I will prove once and for all that I am the fastest creature alive!"

They lined up, side by side, and Pack Rat waved his tail in the air and brought it down to the ground with a snap! Off went Rabbit like a shot! He cleared a path through the tall grass so quickly that it seemed as though a strong wind were blowing.

He ran for a long way before he looked back to see how far ahead of Frog he was. Out of the corner of his eye, he saw Frog jump out of the grass right beside him! Then the next frog leaped ahead of him and disappeared into the grass. After that, the next frog took his long leap, and so on down the line, all the way to the river.

Rabbit didn't realize what was happening and thought that it was the same frog he had started the race with. He twitched his nose, laid back his long ears, and ran faster than ever before.

"Now I will win!" he said. "No frog can run as fast as this!"

Frog leaped out of the grass, just in front of him. Rabbit became supercharged and flew like an arrow across the ground.

The river was soon in sight and Rabbit gave all that he had to put on a final burst of speed to win. But Frog always seemed to be one jump ahead. At the finish line, it was Frog who leaped into the river shouting, "You are too slow, my friend!"

Rabbit was going too fast to stop and went flying head over heels. He landed in the river with a loud *ker-splash!*

Rabbit was so tired that he was barely able to pull himself out of the water. At last he lay on the bank, completely out of breath, disappointed, and very soggy.

It was a long time before anyone heard Rabbit boast of his ability to run again.

ALEXANDER, THE DWARF & THE TROLL

A Tale From Denmark

ONCE A POOR man named Alexander sat under a tree in the deep forest, eating his meager lunch of porridge and bread. A tiny dwarf with a bent back and a long white beard walked up and asked, "Could you spare a coin for an old man?"

"Spare coins I have none," said Alexander politely, "but you're welcome to share my meal."

The dwarf was hungry and quickly ate half the food. Then he tipped his strange-looking hat, clapped his old knarled hands together, and vanished!

Alexander soon heard a thunderous *stomp, stomp, stomp*! A huge troll wife, as large as she was ugly, was heading straight for him.

"You are in my forest!" she cried angrily.

"I'm just passing through," replied Alexander. "I meant no harm."

"And I mean no harm by eating you!"

"Please don't," cried Alexander. "I have a wife and five children. Think of how sad they'll be if you kill me."

"In that case," boomed the beastly troll, "we will play a game. I will give you three chances to hide from me. If I find you all three times, into my pot you go!"

She turned and walked away. Just as suddenly, the old dwarf appeared and said, "Fear not, Alexander, I'll help you hide."

The dwarf used his ax to chop a large slice of bark from a nearby tree. Then he pushed Alexander inside the tree and put the bark back in place.

Soon the troll wife came by carrying a huge ax on her shoulder and muttering, "Ahhh, going to chop down a tree, going to chop down a tree."

She walked right up to Alexander's tree, cut it down with one blow, and pulled him out.

"You lose once," she laughed. And off she went.

The dwarf again appeared and said, "We can't let her win so easily. Come with me."

He took Alexander to the edge of the forest. There they found a lake thick with hollow reeds. The dwarf pulled a reed from the mud and tapped Alexander on the shoulder with it. He was instantly reduced to the size of an ant! The dwarf put him inside the reed and stuck it back into the mud.

Before long the troll came by carrying a large knife. She was muttering, "Ahhh, going to cut the reeds, going to cut the reeds."

After she sliced the reeds down, she picked them up and gave them a hard shake. *PLOP!* Alexander fell to the ground and returned to his normal size.

"That's twice you lose," she laughed. "Next time I'll shake you into my pot." Away she went.

Alexander started to cry. The dwarf appeared and said, "Cheer up! We still have a chance."

He clapped his hands together and Alexander turned into a large fish flopping on the ground. The dwarf tossed him into the lake and said, "Swim away, my friend."

The troll wife walked up carrying a huge washtub on her back and a fishing pole over her shoulder. "Ahhh, going to catch a fish, going to catch a fish."

She put the tub into the water and climbed inside. Then she pushed off from shore and cast her line.

The dwarf stood on the lake's edge and blew out three huge breaths. A storm arose and the wind howled across the choppy water. Monstrous waves whirled the washtub this way and that, and the troll began to yell for mercy! The tub tipped over, and down, down to the bottom of the lake the troll sank, never to reappear.

The wind died down and the water became calm. The fish swam to shore and the dwarf clapped his hands together twice. Alexander was himself once again.

"Thank you for sharing your lunch, Alexander," said the dwarf, and he was gone.

Alexander went home and told his family the story of his narrow escape. Never again did he see the dwarf.

MEDICINE WOLF

A Native American Tale

⊙HE BLACKFOOT INDIANS were moving from the summer to the winter camp one year, long ago. As they went, they were attacked by a band of Crow warriors, and several of the Blackfoot were killed. A young woman of the tribe, named Sits-By-The-Door, was taken as a slave.

She was tied to a horse and taken to the Crow camp on the Yellowstone River. Sits-By-The-Door was made to do the hardest jobs, and if ever she complained, she was kicked and given no food to eat. The man who had captured her tied her up at night and made her sleep next to his wife. But the wife had a good heart and tried to show kindness to Sits-By-The-Door. Although they spoke diffcrent tongues, both understood sign language. One day the wife told Sits-By-The-Door that the warriors had decided to kill her. She had to escape that night.

When her husband was sleeping soundly, the wife cut the rawhide thongs from Sits-By-The-Door's hands and feet. She gave her a small bag of dried meat called pemmican and told her to travel far and fast, for the warriors would surely try to capture her in the morning.

Sits-By-The-Door ran and walked and ran again until the sun began to rise. Exhausted, she crawled into a small cave and fell asleep. She stayed hidden for three days more. At last the Crow warriors gave up the search. She was free.

By this time, Sits-By-The-Door's strength, as well as her food, were nearly gone. She began the long journey home with little more than a strong heart. Even worse, she discovered that she was being followed by a large gray wolf.

Sits-By-The-Door walked for two nights and a day before falling to the cold ground, ready to die. The wolf had followed well behind her, patiently awaiting this moment. He approached her cautiously and sniffed at her hands. Sits-By-The-Door could smell his unwashed fur and the stink of his breath. She prayed for a quick death. To her great amazement, the wolf didn't sink his yellow teeth into her throat. Rather, he lay down beside her to keep her warm and safe. In the morning he ran away, only to return a short while later dragging half of a freshly killed buffalo calf. Sits-By-The-Door cooked the meat and shared it with the wolf. By the following day, she had regained her strength.

The wolf walked beside her for the remainder of the journey home. When she came into the Blackfoot camp, the People were excited to see her and impressed with her new friend. She told them how the wolf had saved her life, and added, "There is strong medicine between us. I call him Medicine Wolf."

The People understood her words. They believed in the magic bond or "medicine" that can exist between an animal and a human. The council of elders decided that the wolf could stay in the village and live with Sits-By-The-Door. Even the camp dogs had to leave the wolf in peace. He stayed with his human friend until she died, many years later. Then he left the village and was never seen again.

SEÑOR RATTLESNAKE LEARNS TO FLY

A Tale From Mexico

ONCE, SEÑOR RATTLESNAKE spoke with two buzzards sitting on a rock in the middle of the desert.

"I am tired of always having to slither across the hot sand on my belly. I want to fly through the air like both of you. How wonderful it must feel to float high above the world! I may be a snake in body, but in my heart I'm a bird!"

The buzzards felt sorry for the rattlesnake and tried to cheer him up. "Flying is nice, Brother Snake," said the younger bird, "but so is being on the ground. You can't take a nap while up in the sky."

"How true," agreed the other buzzard, "and besides, everyone fears you on the ground, Señor Rattlesnake. You rule the sand."

"But I want to fly," replied the snake. "Just once, I want to feel the wind at my tail, and I want to see my entire kingdom from the air."

The buzzards thought long and hard on the problem. At last the older said, "Although it is impossible for you to fly like a bird, perhaps we could take you for a ride in the sky."

"Si, si!" (which means, "Yes, yes!"), cried the snake. "Which of you will carry me on your back?"

"No, my friend," said the older bird, "you are too heavy for just one of us. There has to be a way for both of us to carry you in flight."

"We could do it with a stick!" exclaimed the young buzzard. "I'll go and find one."

Soon the young bird returned with a long, thin yucca stalk. It had dried out in the sun and was both lightweight and strong. Each bird took one end of

the stalk in his mouth and, together, they perched on the rock. Señor Rattlesnake slithered up the side of the rock and joined them at the top.

"Bite the middle of the stick with your long fangs, Brother Snake, and hold on tight!" said the older buzzard.

The birds slowly flapped their large black wings and rose high into the air, carrying the stick and Señor Rattlesnake with them. The snake gripped the stick tightly with his fangs as his long body swayed lightly in the air. It was an exhilarating experience! Indeed, it was just what he had always hoped for.

Just then, Señor Eagle happened to fly by and decided to have some fun with his old enemy. "Why not flap your wings, Brother Snake? Those are strange feathers growing from your tail! Do you always fly with a stick in your mouth?" taunted Señor Eagle.

Then a small dove perched right on the yucca stalk, close to the snake's head, and said, "Don't be angry, Señor Snake. Eagle wants you to open your mouth and fall to the ground."

The snake gave the dove an evil look and, for a moment, forgot where he was. His true nature took over and he opened his mouth wide to strike the dove.

Down, down, down he fell, twisting and turning and flying through the air faster than he believed was possible. He landed in the middle of a prickly pear cactus with a hard thud!

It took several days for Señor Rattlesnake to recover from his adventure, and with every cactus spine he plucked from his scales, he cared less and less about flying.

GRANDFATHER SPIDER'S FEAST

A Tale From Africa

ONE DAY GRANDFATHER Spider watched with interest as the bees collected an enormous amount of golden pollen from the flowers with which to make honey. "Why so much honey?" he asked.

"For the feast, the feast," buzzed the bees.

"What feast? When is it? Where will it be?" asked Grandfather Spider impatiently.

The bees were too busy to answer all of his questions and went on with their work.

"I'll ask the ants," said Grandfather to himself. "They know everything that is happening around here."

He ran through the jungle undergrowth as fast as his eight legs could carry his fat body, and soon arrived at the ant hill. The army of ants was marching in long lines, some going out into the jungle and others returning to the colony. And every ant was carrying a grain of rice, a juicy green leaf, a tasty mushroom, or a sweet berry.

"Why so much food?" asked Grandfather.

"For the feast, the feast," said the ants.

"Whose feast? Where will it be? When will it be?" he demanded.

The ants went marching on, too busy to answer silly questions.

Grandfather ran to the tree in which he lived and scurried up the trunk. There he spun a heavy web between two branches and, using a twig wrapped with soft leaves, began drumming a message to his many grandchildren scattered throughout the jungle.

"Come home at once, come home at once ... Your grandfather wants you to come home at once...."

Quickly the message traveled and just as quickly little spiders came rushing from every corner of the jungle to see what their grandfather wanted.

"Who is having a feast? When and where will it be held?" asked Grandfather Spider.

"It is Lion, Grandfather," said a spider from the east side of the jungle. "He is having a wedding party in two or three days."

"It is Elephant, Grandfather," said a spider from the jungle's west side. "She is celebrating her birthday sometime next week."

"It is Monkey, Grandfather," said a spider from the north side of the jungle. "He is having a feast for his friends in just a few days."

"It is Zebra, Grandfather," said a spider from the southern edge of the jungle. "She is celebrating the birth of her baby."

"What?" exclaimed Grandfather, "Four feasts in the same week? How exciting! How delicious! But which one will begin first? Should I travel east, west, north, or south?"

Grandfather Spider thought for a moment and then began to spin four long, silken threads. He tied one end of each of the threads around his fat middle, and gave each of the four spiders who had told him of the feasts one end each.

"Tie these threads to your waists, just as I have done, and then go back to your homes. Whenever one of you hears that a party is beginning, pull hard on the thread and I will know in which direction to travel. With any luck, I should be able to attend all four!"

The little spiders agreed that it was a wonderful plan and went back to their homes in the four corners of the jungle. Grandfather awaited the first tug by going to sleep and dreaming about food.

Two days later a drum was heard in the East announcing Lion's party. The little spider yanked on the thread tied to his waist. Just then another drum sounded in the West for elephant's celebration, and the Western Spider pulled on his thread. Suddenly, a drum pounded in the North as Monkey's feast was beginning. The third spider tugged hard on his thread. Within a few minutes, Zebra announced the start of her party with the Southern drums. Of course, that spider yanked on her thread as well.

Grandfather yelled, "Ouch! I'm going east! Oooh, it's west! Ahh, it's north! Nooo, it's south … *Stop! Everyone stop pulling! You're squeezing me in half! Please stop*!"

His grandchildren were too far away to hear his cries, and as they pulled harder and harder, the threads grew tighter and tighter, and Grandfather's fat waist grew smaller and smaller, until at last, all four silken threads snapped!

Now Grandfather Spider's big waist was tiny, and so it has remained to this very day.

THE MIRROR

A Tale From Korea

A LARGE FAMILY of farmers lived in the country. There was a young husband and wife in this family, and the husband had to go to town on business. His wife asked, "Will you buy me a comb for my hair?"

"Anything for you, dear wife," he replied.

Now the wife knew that her husband was absent-minded, and wanted him to remember the comb. A new moon shone in the sky that night, just a thin crescent of light. It was the perfect shape of the comb she desired. She said to him, "Look at the moon, husband. It is just like the comb I want. If you forget, look at the moon and you'll remember."

The young man was in town for weeks, and was completely occupied with business matters. Naturally, he forgot all about the comb. When it came time to return home, he happened to look up into the night sky. The moon was no longer the crescent shape of a comb, but rather a full round sphere of yellow light.

"What is it that I'm supposed to bring to my wife?" the young farmer asked himself. "Something shaped like the moon...."

He went to a shopkeeper and said, "I want to buy something that is round like the moon, something my wife would like."

The shopkeeper looked around his shop and said, "This mirror is round. Your wife would like to see herself in it."

Mirrors were quite rare in Korea at this long-ago time, and the young husband had never seen one before. He bought it and walked the long road back to the farm. The moon was rising in the night sky when he arrived. He gave the mirror to his wife. She looked into the glass and saw the reflection of a pretty young woman.

"Eeehhh!" she cried. "I ask for a comb and my husband brings home a young woman."

Her mother was in the room, and she looked into the mirror. Of course she saw her own wrinkled face, and said, "Silly daughter, this is no young woman. This is an old and honorable woman. Perhaps it is his mother."

"You are wrong," the wife said. "It is a pretty *young* woman."

"No, you are wrong," the mother replied. "Look! She's a white-haired *old* woman!"

As the two women argued, a small boy who was eating a rice cake came into the room. He picked up the mirror and saw another boy eating a rice cake. The boy thought that the stranger had stolen his food. "Return my rice cake!" he shouted. He raised his fist and shook it at the stranger. The stranger shook his fist right back. The boy was frightened and he began to cry.

The noise of the women arguing and the boy crying brought the grandfather running into the room. "What's wrong?" he asked.

The boy said that a stranger had stolen his rice cake. The grandfather became angry and said, "Show me the scoundrel. No one steals from my grandson and gets away with it!" He grabbed the mirror and saw an enraged old man with fire in his eyes.

"Listen old man," said Grandfather. "You should be ashamed of yourself for stealing from a boy. I'm going to teach you a lesson!"

He made a fist and punched his image in the glass. The mirror crashed to the floor! Grandfather, grandmother, the boy, the wife, and the husband stared with amazement at the broken bits of glass scattered all over the room.

"I think the thief is gone," said the boy.

"And I think I'll let my wife do her own shopping from now on," said the husband.

"I'll get the broom," said Grandmother.

The wife stepped out on the porch and looked up at the night sky. It may have just been a cloud passing by, but it looked to her as though the moon winked!

DAMON & PYTHIAS

A Tale From Ancient Greece

LONG, LONG AGO, a powerful king named Dionysius ruled the island of Sicily. Dionysius was as cruel as he was strong and had made many enemies among the Greeks. He was, therefore, constantly afraid of being assassinated.

His fears were justified. A young Greek named Pythias plotted to murder the tyrant and free Sicily of his dictatorship. Pythias was caught before he could carry out his plan, however, and sentenced to die.

"Have you anything to say before you meet the executioner?" asked King Dionysius.

"Yes," said Pythias. "I would ask that you grant me five days more. My parents live many miles to the west. They are old and have little. I want to settle my affairs, sell my house, and take the money to them. It would ease the pain of their final years and I could say good-bye as a son should."

"How do I know that you will return in five days?" asked the king. "It would seem logical that you would flee this country and try to save your miserable life."

"You have my word," answered Pythias.

"I do not trust the word of an assassin," said Dionysius. "I must have someone to take your place. Someone who will volunteer to give his life to the executioner if you do not return at the appointed hour. Have you such a friend as this?"

"Yes," said Pythias.

"Yes," echoed a young man as he stepped forward from the crowd of watchers. "My name is Damon, friend to Pythias. I will stay in his cell until he returns and, if need be, I will die for him."

"You are a foolish friend," said Dionysius, "for I will not hesitate to order your death at sunset, five days from now, if Pythias isn't here."

Pythias ran to his house and made the necessary arrangements to have it sold. He then settled his affairs and, after two of the five precious days had passed, began the long walk to the village of his childhood. It took one day more to reach the river and cross the bridge that led to his parents' cottage. The fourth day was spent in sadness, for his mother and father were heartbroken. Even the skies wept that night, and a heavy rain fell for hours. On the morning of his final day, Pythias walked a muddy path back to the river.

His heart sank when he arrived at water's edge. The bridge had washed away during the storm. The current was too swift to risk swimming and there were no boats at hand. He couldn't get to the other side.

When the sun had reached its peak, Dionysius had Damon brought from his cell.

"Your friend is not going to come and save you," said the king. "Perhaps I should kill you now."

"Pythias will be here before the sun sets," Damon calmly replied.

Three more hours passed, and still Pythias had not arrived.

"You were a fool to take his place!" cried the king. "See? He loves his own life more than yours!"

"You are wrong, Your Majesty," said Damon. "He loves me even more than I love him. He will come."

Two hours later, Damon was led to the chopping block.

"You see? He failed you," said Dionysius scornfully, "just as I said he would."

"I trust him even now," said Damon.

The executioner raised his cruel ax high into the air, but before he could strike the fatal blow, a voice was heard in the distance: "Set Damon free! I'm here!"

44

Pythias ran into the town square and collapsed at the king's feet. He had run downriver for many miles to find another bridge to cross.

"I'm here," he gasped. "Let my friend go free."

Dionysius found himself strangely moved. "Never have I seen such a friendship as between Damon and Pythias. Neither shall die! Their friendship must be allowed to live."

THE PRINCESS WHO COULD NOT CRY

An Original Tale, More or Less

There are many stories about young princesses who couldn't laugh, but have you ever heard one about a princess who could not cry? I hadn't either, and I thought it time that there was one. Here it is:

A BEAUTIFUL PRINCESS always laughed, even when she was sad. An evil fairy had placed a curse upon her at birth and the royal child simply could not cry. Thus she laughed at everything—which often proved to be embarrassing.

Desperate, the queen called upon a wise gypsy and asked for her advice. The old woman gazed into a crystal ball for a long moment and then said, with a voice as ancient as time, "If the princess can be made to cry just once, the spell will be broken forever. She will then be able to cry like a normal person."

The king offered a rich reward of land and gold to anyone who could make his daughter cry—without hurting her.

Several people arrived at the castle gate with clever solutions. One woman told tragic stories and sang sad songs for two days and two nights. The princess stayed as happy as a hummingbird, although she was a bit tired.

An unpleasant-looking man made horrid faces scary enough to frighten any child to tears. The princess laughed and laughed and begged for more.

One of the king's counselors suggested that the royal daughter be forced to throw her favorite toys down from the tallest tower. The princess smiled as she gathered up her finest dolls, and giggled as she carried them up the winding staircase to the top of the highest tower. She hooted and hollered as she tossed them over the side, one by one, and watched them smash to pieces on the stone walkway so very far below.

The king and queen were beside themselves with grief and wept loudly for their daughter. She heard them sobbing and couldn't keep herself from laughing even harder.

One bright morning soon after, a ragged little girl with a dirty face carried a small basket to the castle door. Her name was Gillian and she lived deep in the forest with her old mother. They were as poor as scarecrows, and just as skinny. To make matters worse, Gillian's mother had fallen terribly ill. The little girl pulled bravely on the bell rope and a guard opened the heavy wooden door.

"I've come to make the princess cry," said Gillian with a small, frightened voice.

The guard escorted her inside. The queen looked upon Gillian with kindness and said, "Promise me you won't hurt her."

"I promise, Your Majesty."

Gillian was taken to the princess's room and left alone with her. News of the child's visit quickly spread throughout the castle, and a small crowd of counselors, noblemen and women, kitchen and stable help, all joined the queen outside the princess's door. It wasn't long before they heard the amazing sound of two little girls sniffling. Then they heard quiet weeping, which soon changed to loud bawling!

The queen could stand it no longer and threw open the door. What a surprise it turned out to be! Gillian and the princess sat on the floor with the poor girl's basket between them. Each held a paring knife in one hand and a large, ripe onion in the other. Gillian was showing the princess how to peel it. Wet tears streamed down both their faces. At long last, the princess was crying, really crying!

The evil spell had been broken and the royal child could now laugh when she was happy and cry when she was sad. Gillian was given the land and the gold, and lived in comfort with her old mother, who, you will be happy to know, was now quite well.

The best part was that Gillian's land was right next to the castle, and she and the princess played together nearly every day. Sometimes, even many years later, the two could be seen crying together in the kitchen of the castle as they made onion soup. For the princess had grown quite fond of onions since that fateful day when she learned how to cry.

THE LION'S WHISKER

A Tale From Africa

ONCE THERE LIVED a husband and wife in a small village in Ethiopia. The husband was not happy with the marriage and usually came home late from his work in the fields. Sometimes he failed to come home at all.

His wife loved him, but she was just as unhappy in the relationship, and finally went to talk with the oldest and wisest man in the village. The old man had married them two years before and now she asked him to end the marriage.

The village elder listened patiently to her bitter words and responded with kindness. "Separation isn't always the best choice. I know of a better way. I will prepare a secret potion that will change your husband into an obedient and loving man. He will come home on time and try always to please you."

"Prepare this wonderful medicine at once!" cried the woman. For truly, she wanted to stay married.

"Ah, that's not an easy thing to do," replied the wise man. "I lack one vital ingredient, a single whisker taken from a living lion. If you can bring me such a whisker, I will make the potion."

"I'll get it for you," she said with determination.

The following morning, the woman carried a large chunk of raw meat down to the river where the lion often came to drink. Hiding behind a clump of bushes, she waited quietly until the lion appeared. The woman was frightened and wanted to run away, but found the courage to toss the meat to the hungry beast. He devoured it in three gulps and walked slowly back into the trees. The woman fed the lion again the next morning and every morning that week. During the second week she began to creep out of hiding and let the lion see who was bringing his breakfast. By the third week she began to move closer and closer to the feeding lion, and when four weeks had passed she was able to sit down quietly next to him while he ate. Thus it became possible, one day, for her to gently reach over and pluck a single whisker from his chin.

She ran to the wise man with the prize and pleaded with him to make the secret potion at once! He was surprised to see the whisker and demanded to know how she acquired it.

Upon hearing the tale, the old man said, "You do not need magic to change the ways of your husband. You are brave enough to pull a single whisker from a living lion. It was a dangerous task which required cleverness, courage, and patience. If you can accomplish this, then can you not use that same courage, wit, and patience to improve your marriage?

"Don't get angry with your husband, but show him each day that you do, indeed, love him. Gently point out that you, too, are to be respected and loved. Share his problems and make him feel wanted. Give him time to change and see what will happen."

The woman went home and put the advice to work. Slowly but surely, the relationship began to improve. Within a year their life together grew into one of happiness which lasted for a lifetime.

HOW THE MOSQUITOS LEFT KAMBARA

A Tale From Fiji

ONCE LONG AGO, a small island in the Pacific called Kambara was infested with mosquitoes. The island people were constantly at war with the pesky insects and grew weary of being bitten, especially at night. All day long the women of the tribe pounded tree bark into fine-mesh screens to keep the mosquitoes out.

Now it happened that a prince from the island of Oneata sailed throughout the South Pacific in search of treasures for his people. He landed on Kambara and the chief welcomed him as an honored guest. After a great feast, the prince was shown to a sleeping room. It was surrounded with beautifully painted mosquito screens.

"Tell me, O Chief of Kambara," said the prince, "why do you hang such wonderful cloth all about the room?"

"For the mosquitoes," replied the chief.

"Mosquitoes? What are mosquitoes?" asked the prince.

"Our little … friends of the night. They are small flying insects that … sing us to sleep each night," said the chief. He was too embarrassed to tell the truth.

"How nice," said the prince. "We have nothing like mosquitoes on Oneata."

"Too bad," said the chief. "We have more than we need."

The prince yawned, and just as he began to fall asleep, the night air filled with the hum and buzz of thousands of hungry mosquitoes flying outside the curtain. "Such a soothing sound," The muttered. "A rare treasure, indeed."

The next morning the prince asked the chief if he could take some mosquitoes back to Oneata with him.

"You would have to take *all* of them," replied the chief, "since they are a close-knit family and couldn't stand to be separated."

"But what about your people?" asked the worried prince. "Wouldn't they be unhappy if I took *all* of your lovely mosquitoes?"

"Yes, they would," replied the chief, "but if you were to give us something in return, I think they would be satisfied."

"I have a magic conch shell in my canoe," said the eager prince. "You blow it like a trumpet and the fish swim to shore and let themselves be caught. Your people will never grow hungry!"

"It's a bargain," said the chief of Kambara happily. "Our mosquitoes for your magic shell!"

The people of Kambara set a trap for the mosquitoes, using a huge basket so tightly woven that even the smallest of the insects couldn't get out. They placed a freshly killed pig in the basket and the chief waited behind a nearby tree with the lid.

The sun began to set and the mosquitoes came out in droves in search of victims. Some of the pests found the pig, and it wasn't long before every mosquito on the island was in the basket enjoying the feast. The chief jumped out from behind the tree, popped the lid on the basket, and tied it securely with long vines.

With the basket in his canoe, the prince sailed back to Oneata. He thought of how happy his people would be with the restful sounds of the mosquitoes.

The chief of Kambara was also happy. He blew on the conch shell and the islanders began gathering in the fish for a celebration feast!

CLEVER GRETEL

A Tale From Germany

ONCE UPON A time, a cook named Gretel worked for the town mayor. One day the mayor said, "Prepare two fine hens for dinner, Gretel, as I'm expecting an important guest."

Gretel went to the market and bought two fat birds, already plucked. Once home, she stuffed them with raisins and bread crumbs, basted them with melted butter, and began roasting them over a slow fire. Before long they were nicely browned and smelled delicious. But she couldn't serve them for the guest hadn't yet arrived.

"It's a shame they can't be eaten right now," said Gretel to herself. "They are so hot and tender and juicy. I'll bet they are tasty! But one can't always tell just by looking. I'll have to take a bite, just a little nibble so the mayor won't know."

She pulled off one of the wings and quickly devoured it. "Oh my, but that is good! Why, it's one of the best hens I've ever cooked. But the bird looks funny with only one wing sticking out. I'd better eat the other one too, so the mayor won't notice anything wrong."

After she had eaten the second wing, she called to the mayor to see if his guest had arrived.

"Not yet," he replied from the other room.

"Oh dear, the birds are getting cold. I can't put them back into the oven or they'll burn to a crisp. Maybe his guest isn't coming after all. I suppose it would be all right to eat the rest of the hen while it's still hot."

She devoured the chicken, enjoying each savory bite. Indeed, she thought it so delicious that she pulled a wing from the second bird to see if it tasted equally good. "Oh my, it's even better!"

Before Gretel realized it, she had eaten the second hen as well. As she wiped the grease from her chin, the mayor called.

"Hurry, Gretel! I can see my guest coming up the path."

"Yes ... Mister Mayor," she said hesitantly. "I'll serve dinner ... in a moment..."

The mayor enjoyed the task of carving birds and he began to sharpen his largest butcher knife on a stone.

A gentle knock at the kitchen door announced the guest's arrival. He had come to the back door by mistake. Gretel opened it just a crack and said, "Quickly, run for your life! The mayor asked you to dinner, but actually he plans to cut off your ears! Listen, you can hear him sharpening his knife in the outer room."

The man was shocked and said, "Thank you for the warning." Then he ran back down the path toward the roadway.

Gretel called to the mayor, "Hurry, Your Honor, your guest has just stolen the hens and is running away with them!"

"Didn't he leave one for me?" cried the mayor.

"No, he took the pair," she said.

Holding the carving knife above his head, the mayor ran after his guest and yelled, "I only want one! Do you hear? It's only one that I want!"

The poor mayor only wanted one of the delicious birds, but the guest thought that he wanted only one of his ears. So he kept on running!

AH SHUNG CATCHES A GHOST

A Tale From China

AH SHUNG WAS both brave and clever, and one night he decided to catch a ghost. He waited until the moon was floating high in the dark sky and then walked quietly along the path leading to the deepest part of the forest.

He saw a shadow slip out from behind a tree. Then a cold finger touched his shoulder. A whispery voice said, "Excuse me, but do you know the way to town?"

In spite of his courage, Ah Shung had goosebumps. "Who are you?" he asked.

"A ghost, of course," came the quiet reply. "And who are you?"

"Oh, I'm a ghost too," lied Ah Shung, "and since I'm on my way to town, why don't you join me?"

"Excellent," said the ghost, and he began floating alongside the man. "Whom are you planning to scare tonight?"

"I haven't decided yet," said Ah Shung, who was beginning to sweat. "I'll wait to see who is still up at this late hour. How about you?"

The ghost chuckled and said, "Well, there is a fellow named Ah Shung, and I've been meaning to scare him for some time. Yes, I'll look him up tonight. How far is it to town?"

"About th-th-three miles," Ah Shung stuttered.

"Let's take turns carrying each other," suggested the ghost. "It will make the journey go faster."

"All right," said Ah Shung, and he climbed onto the ghost's back.

The phantom carried him for a mile, complaining all the way, "You're the heaviest ghost I've ever met."

"I died just last week," explained Ah Shung. "New ghosts are always heavy."

When the ghost grew too tired to carry the man any further, they exchanged places. The phantom weighed no more than a feather pillow. They came to a shallow river and Ah Shung began to wade across, splashing loudly with each step.

"Why do you make so much noise when you walk?" asked the ghost.

"Because I'm new at being dead," answered Ah Shung, who was growing less and less afraid of the ghost. "Tell me," he continued, "what is it that we ghosts must fear the most from humans?"

"Spit!" cried the ghost. "If a human spits on us, we lose our power to escape."

A short time later, they came within sight of the town. The ghost asked for directions to Ah Shung's house. His companion said, "Follow me. I know his house well, for I used to live in this town."

They arrived at Ah Shung's outer gate and the ghost said, "Watch closely and I'll show you a good way to scare humans."

The phantom quickly changed himself into a horse and said, "I'll walk into his room and complain about the poor quality of oats he feeds his animals. A talking horse should frighten him out of his wits!"

"An excellent idea," cried Ah Shung, as he leaped up onto the ghost-horse's back and spit on his neck! "Ah Shung can use a talking horse to help with all his farm work, even if he does complain about the oats!"

Thus the ghost was caught and remained a horse for several years.

It is said that a ghost is no match for a clever man.

COYOTE STEALS SPRING

A Native American Tale, From the Pacific Northwest

ONCE LONG BEFORE, the cold snows of winter covered the land for ten long months each year, while the warm summer days lasted only a few short weeks. The People gathered whatever food they could find during the short season, but it was never enough to last all winter long. Painful cries of hunger were heard in every lodge.

Coyote, cleverest of all animals, was hungry too, and decided to bring back the season called Spring. Old Woman was the keeper of seasons and she lived in a lodge many miles to the north. She liked Winter best and kept Spring, Summer and Autumn tied up in elkskin bags for most of the year.

Coyote called the People together and asked for Quiet One, Strong Arm, and Sharp Knives to travel with him to Old Woman's lodge. Quiet One and Strong Arm stepped forward. Just then a mighty growl was heard at the edge of the forest and Grizzly Bear stood on his hind legs. He waved his paws, showing off his long, sharp claws.

"Sharp Knives has arrived," said Coyote, "and our journey begins. Quiet One will bring a handful of tree sap and Strong Arm will carry our food."

Coyote, Quiet One, Strong Arm, and Sharp Knives walked northward for several days until at last they saw an ancient lodge on top of a mountain.

"It is the home of Old Woman," whispered Coyote. "Quiet One, you enter the lodge and melt the tree sap over the fire. Pretend you are warming your hands. When the sap grows soft and sticky, ask Old Woman which of the three bags holds Spring. She will point it out and then begin to talk. She is a loud talker and her words can hold you prisoner.

"Stop her words by forcing the sap into her mouth. She will not be able to speak and you can toss the elkskin bag outside."

"I understand, friend Coyote," said Quiet One.

"Strong Arm," continued Coyote, "you pick up the bag and throw it far down the mountainside. Old Woman can run fast."

"I will throw it far," said Strong Arm.

"What is my job?" growled Sharp Knives.

"To catch the bag thrown by Strong Arm and rip it apart with your sharp claws," explained Coyote.

"Yes," grunted Grizzly Bear, "I will do that."

Quiet One and Strong Arm climbed the mountain and approached the lodge. Quiet One slipped inside and began to warm his hands over the crackling fire. The tree sap began to soften.

Old Woman sat looking into the fire, waiting for her visitor to speak. When the sap was warm and sticky, Quiet One asked which of the three elkskin bags held Spring. She pointed to the one nearest him. Then she opened her old mouth wide to begin her loud talking. Without hesitation, Quiet One jammed the sap in and held it there in spite of her struggles.

When it was stuck tight he jumped up, grabbed the bag, and tossed it outside! Old Woman leaped for it, but Strong Arm was quick and heaved it far down the mountainside. Old Woman ran after it, but Sharp Knives caught it and ripped it apart!

The warm winds of Spring were set free. A bright sun appeared in the sky chasing the gray clouds of Winter far away. At long last, Spring had come again.

THE CHIRIMÍA

A Tale From Guatemala

THOUSANDS OF YEARS ago, there lived a Mayan Indian king who had a beautiful daughter. Her name was Princess Nima-cux and she was a happy child. As she grew older, however, she grew mysteriously sad. The king loved his daughter and tried to make her laugh again. He gave her gifts of precious stones and arranged entertainments by the finest musicians in the land, but nothing made her smile. The king consulted his advisors.

"She is of the age to marry, O noble King. If she marries happily, her sadness will vanish," they said.

The king proclaimed that Princess Nima-cux would choose her own husband. He asked all the noblemen to visit and show off their strength and skills. It would also help, he added, if they were handsome.

Dressed in finely woven cloth, gold, and feathers, thirty-three young men arrived on the appointed day. Each displayed his talent in contests of skill, intellect, and art, but none satisfied the princess. In fact, she didn't smile even once.

At the end of the day a young nobleman from the poorest family arrived. He was simply dressed and had a kind face. His treasure was his voice, his gift was his song. The princess smiled for the first time in a year. His was the sweetest voice she had ever heard. The king dismissed all the other suitors and asked the singer to stay for dinner. During the feast, the young man asked for Nima-cux's hand in marriage.

"I will marry you," she said, "when you can sing as sweetly and purely as the songbirds."

"Then I must learn the secrets of the birds," said the youth. "Please give me four months to study."

The princess agreed, and the young nobleman set off, traveling deep into the forest. There he stayed, listening to the birds sing, and trying to sound like them. He practiced day and night, but after three months he was ready to give up. His singing would never match the natural sweetness of the birds. He was so sad that he cried.

Suddenly the Spirit of the Forest appeared and asked him the reason for his tears. Upon hearing his story, the spirit told him to cut a small branch from a nearby tree and hollow it out. She showed him how to shape it like a tube and cut finger holes in its side.

"Blow in one end and move your fingers up and down the holes," she said.

He tried it and the true sound of a songbird came from the stick!

"This is a *chirimia*,"* said the Spirit of the Forest. "Learn to play it well before returning to your princess." She vanished just as suddenly as she had arrived.

The forest was alive with the music from his chirimía all during the last month of his apprenticeship. The nobleman practiced for hours each day by listening to the birds sing and then duplicating their pure sounds on his stick flute.

On the final day he traveled back to the palace and played his new songs. Princess Nima-cux was entranced and said they were the sweetest of all sounds, even those of the songbirds. Filled with joy, they were married the following day.

Ever since that time, the Maya have carved and played the chirimía.

*Chirimía: Pronounced "*chee-ree-MEE-ah*." A Guatemalan wind instrument similar to an oboe.

NATURAL HABITS

A Tale From Africa

LONG AGO IN the deep jungle, Monkey and Rabbit were sharing a meal. Monkey was feasting on ripe yellow bananas while Rabbit munched on juicy green leaves.

While they ate, each practiced the habits most natural to him. Monkey scratched; first his head, then his chest, then his arms and, of course, his legs. He scratched and scratched during the entire meal.

While Monkey scratched, Rabbit turned his head; first to the right, then to the left, then behind him, and then above. He was on the lookout for an enemy attack, and not once during the meal did he refrain from looking about.

Finally Monkey said, "Please stop turning away from me when I'm talking. It's not polite."

"Look who's complaining about good manners," said Rabbit. "You've been scratching the whole time. Scratching is more impolite than looking for enemies."

"Then I'll stop scratching," said Monkey. "It's easy for me to keep still."

"It's just as easy for me to stop looking," said Rabbit. "In fact, I'll bet that I can keep still longer than you can."

"I'll bet you can't," said Monkey. "And the loser will feed the winner for a week."

"Agreed!" cried Rabbit. "The first to move loses."

So they sat facing each other, neither scratching nor looking about. Ten minutes went by, then ten more. Both grew anxious, but neither moved. When thirty minutes had elapsed, the situation had become unbearable. Monkey itched so badly that he felt like screaming! Rabbit was so frightened of his enemies that he was trembling!

Finally Monkey said, "Let's tell each other stories to pass the time."

"All right," said Rabbit. "You go first."

"My story," began Monkey, "is about the time that I got separated from my mother when I was just three months old. I was too young to be in the jungle all alone and I nearly got killed.

"First, I got hit on the head by a falling branch. It was small, but you should have seen the lump on my head. It was right here...." He rubbed his head with his paw, scratching at the terrible itch. "Then I ran into a hornet's nest and got stung on my chest, and here on my arms..." Of course he scratched away those itches as well.

"I tried to run away, but tripped over a vine and nearly broke my leg. I had a big swelling right here...." *Scratch, scratch, scratch.*

Rabbit realized that Monkey was trying to trick him and said, "Now I'll tell a story. One night when I was young, my mother went on an errand and told me to keep watch over my many brothers and sisters. It was so dark that even the moon stayed hidden behind the clouds, and I jumped at every jungle sound.

"First, I heard a twig snap somewhere to my right...." He used the opportunity to look to his right. "Then I heard a strange cry coming from somewhere on my left...." His head spun to the left.

"Soon a large bird fluttered its wings behind me...." He looked behind. "But just then something fell from the trees above...." And up into the sky he looked.

Monkey began laughing and said, "I guess we can't change the habits that are natural to us."

"No," laughed Rabbit, "we can't. The bet is off. We will just have to feed ourselves for the next week."

THE MAGIC POT

A Tale From China

ONCE A POOR but hardworking woodcutter was walking home from the forest, with an ax strapped to his back. Suddenly he came upon a large old pot made of brass. It was the biggest pot he had ever seen.

"What a fine pot!" he exclaimed. "But how will I get it home? It's too heavy to carry … Wait, I know…." He untied his shoulder strap and dropped the heavy ax into the pot. He proceeded to tie one end of the strap through one of the pot's handles and the other end around his waist. Then he began the hard work of dragging the clumsy pot down the path to his small house.

The woodcutter's wife was most pleased to see the pot and said, "What a fortunate day, husband. You found a wonderful old pot and another ax."

"No, wife, I just found the pot. I had the ax before."

"But there are two axes in the pot," she said.

The woodcutter looked inside and was speechless. Two identical axes sat side by side. As he leaned down to pull them out, his straw hat fell from his head and into the pot. Now two hats rested near the axes.

"Wife! The pot is haunted!"

"Or it's magical!" she said happily. "Let's put tonight's dinner inside and see what happens."

One dinner became two.

"Quickly," said the wife. "Get our savings from the jar on the shelf!"

The handful of coins doubled.

"It is magical!" cried the woodcutter. "What shall we put in next?"

"The money, of course," said his practical wife. "Let's get rich while we can."

They placed the coins inside repeatedly, and the amount doubled each time. An hour later every jar, pan, basket, pocket, chest, shelf, and shoe they owned was filled with money. They were, indeed, rich!

"Dear wife," said the woodcutter, "we can build a fine house and have a big vegetable garden, and I won't have to work so hard from now on. I'm so happy that I could dance!"

Then he grabbed her around the waist and began to dance around and around the small room. Suddenly he slipped on some loose coins and accidentally dropped his wife into the pot! He tried to pull her back out—but it was too late. He now had *two* wives. They stepped out of the pot and looked closely at each other. It was impossible to tell them apart.

"What have I done?" cried the woodcutter. "Can a man live with two wives at the same time?"

"Not in my house," said the first wife.

"Not in my house," said the second wife.

Both women smiled and grabbed the woodcutter and made him get into the pot. Two woodcutters climbed back out.

"Can two families live in the same house?" asked both of the men.

"No," said the first wife.

"No," echoed the second wife.

Half the money was given to the second couple and they built an elegant house. It was right next to the first couple's fine, new house. Ever since that time, the people of the village have remarked on the strong resemblance of the woodcutter and his wife's new relatives, the ones who must have brought them all that money!

ADA & THE RASCALS

A Tale From Holland

A FARMER NAMED Johan lived in Holland long ago. Sad to say, he wasn't very intelligent. The smartest thing he ever did was to fall in love with Ada, for she had wit enough for two. They married and settled on a farm in the countryside.

One day Ada told Johan to take their fattest cow to town and sell her for no less than one hundred guilders. (Guilder is the Dutch name for dollar.) He left early in the morning, leading the cow with a rope. About a mile down the road, he passed by an inn where three rascals liked to eat.

"Let's trick Johan out of his cow," said one. "He is stupid and it should be easy to cheat him."

The others agreed and they quickly thought of a plan. All three raced across the field and posted themselves on the road about half a mile apart. When Johan passed by the first rascal, the man said, "What a nice old horse you have there. Are you taking her to town?"

"Are you blind?" asked Johan. "Anyone can see that this is a cow."

Johan kept walking and came to the second fellow who said, "Good day, farmer. That certainly is a fine horse you're leading. Why not ride her?"

"No, no!" said Johan. "This is a cow! Ada said to take the cow to market, and that's what I'm doing."

"I know a horse when I see one," said the scoundrel, and he walked away.

Johan grew worried and thought that perhaps he had made a terrible mistake, but then again, he thought to himself, the animal at the end of the rope looked more like a cow than a horse.

The third joker walked up and said, "Hello, good neighbor. Is your horse for sale?"

"That does it," said Johan to himself. "It's a horse after all."

"I asked if she is for sale," said the rascal, "because I will give you thirty guilders for her."

Johan knew that thirty guilders was a good price for an old horse and said, "It's a bargain."

When the simple man returned home, Ada was furious! She realized that her husband hadn't stood a chance against three clever thieves and decided to teach them a lesson. She went to town early the next morning and set a trap. Then she went home and gave Johan an old brass ring and told him exactly what to do.

Johan began walking to town that afternoon, the ring prominently displayed on his finger. He arrived at the inn and found the three rascals inside. They gladly accepted his offer to buy refreshments. When it came time to pay the bill, Johan held up his hand, twisted the ring on his finger, and asked, "How much do I owe?"

"Nothing," said the innkeeper. "It's all taken care of."

The three men looked at each other in astonishment, but said nothing. They walked with Johan to the next inn and joined him in an expensive meal. After they had eaten their fill, Johan twisted his ring. The second innkeeper rushed to their table and thanked them for coming, adding quietly that the bill was already paid for.

The scoundrels had to know where Johan had found the charmed ring. They kept pestering him with questions until at last he replied, "My wife discovered it in the garden. She said it is worth a fortune."

"We'll give you a hundred guilders for it!" said the lead rascal. "How does that sound?"

"Like a fortune!" said Johan. "It's a bargain."

Johan took the money home and Ada was pleased. "Now we have 130 guilders from those thieves," she explained, "One hundred to pay for the cow and thirty more to pay for the food and drink which I arranged with the innkeepers this morning."

Those three rascals never tried to trick simple Johan again.

THE MISER

A Tale From the United States

A WEALTHY BUT stingy man lived in a big city many long years ago. He was so miserly that he didn't have any friends. He believed that time was far too valuable to waste on others. In truth, he was lonely and unhappy, and, deep in his heart, wanted to change his ways.

One day a poor family moved into his neighborhood and he decided to make friends with them.

"I will give them a gift, a fine gift indeed. But what kind of gift does one give, I wonder?"

He visited his new neighbors and found that the man and wife had three little girls. "I would like to give you a gift in the name of friendship," said the miser, "but you'll have to tell me what you would like."

"Candy!" cried the youngest daughter.

"Cookies!" offered the middle child.

"Cake!" said the oldest.

"Cake it shall be!" said the miser. "And it will be the finest cake that money can buy!"

With their parents' permission, the three girls went with their neighbor to the most expensive bakery in town. The baker had just completed decorating a magnificent chocolate cake, four layers high and covered with a thick white frosting. The girls agreed that this was the most wonderful cake in existence!

The miser asked the price of the cake and turned pale upon hearing the answer. "But," he said to the baker, "how do I know that this really is the best cake in town? Is it, for example, as sweet as honey?"

"Not exactly," explained the baker. "I use sugar in my cakes, not honey."

The miser knew that a pound of honey cost less than the cake. He said, "We want only the best! Come children, we will buy honey instead of a sugar cake."

When they arrived at the beekeeper's shop, the miser asked, "Is your honey as smooth as soft butter?"

"No," answered the beekeeper. "Some of the honeycomb is mixed in with the honey."

The miser knew that butter cost less than honey and said, "We demand the finest. Come children, we will purchase a pound of smooth butter instead of crunchy honey."

At the dairy shop the miser asked, "Is your soft butter as golden in color as the juice of a ripe orange?"

"My butter is yellow in color, not golden," replied the shopmistress.

Realizing that oranges cost less than butter, the miser said, "Only the very best is good enough for us! Come children, we will buy golden orange juice instead of yellow butter."

They walked to the fruit stand and the miser asked, "Is the juice of your sweetest orange as fresh as river water?"

"My juice is fresh," said the merchant, "but water from the river is constantly moving and is the freshest of all."

The miser thought that water would be the absolute best bargain! He said, "We want the finest! Come children, we will drink our fill of fresh river water."

The two youngest girls began to cry, and even though the oldest tried to blink them back, wet tears rolled down her cheeks too. The girls turned away from their neighbor and ran home.

The miser felt a coldness in his heart and a tear gathered at the corner of his eye. He ran back to the bakery, purchased the four-layer cake and carried it to his neighbor's house.

A strange feeling came over him as he knocked on the door ... it was his heart beginning to thaw.

THE BOSUNG POHOO

A Tale From India

A VERY LONG time ago there lived a king who wanted to marry the wife of his prime minister. Her name was Nanda and she was as intelligent as she was beautiful. Nanda was also deeply in love with her husband. But the king was a rascal and he decided that he would have to end the prime minister's life. Then he would make Nanda his queen.

He crafted a wicked plan. A legendary beast called the Bosung Pohoo supposedly lived in the rugged mountains high above the kingdom. Everyone agreed that the animal was a killer and impossible to capture. No one had actually seen the Bosung Pohoo, but just the mention of its name made even the bravest tremble. The king commanded his prime minister to capture the beast alive and bring it to the palace within one month. "If you fail in this task," explained the ruler, "you will lose your head."

The prime minister told his wife of the king's cruelty. "I will die if I go after the Bosung Pohoo, and I will die if I don't. What shall I do, dear Nanda?"

She thought for a long moment and said, "I have a plan. If you follow it, all will be well. Tomorrow morning, announce that you are setting out to find the beast, then ride off into the mountains. Under the cover of darkness return home and I will hide you in the back room. When the month is over, we will have a surprise waiting for the king."

Her husband agreed and, after starting out on the hunt, returned home and stayed hidden for the entire month. At last, the king paid a visit and asked Nanda if she had heard from her husband.

"Oh, My Lord, I'm afraid that he is dead."

"Don't be sad," said the king. "I've always loved you and I want you to be my queen."

Just then there came a loud commotion from the front yard.

"My husband!" cried Nanda. "He has returned at last! You must hide, Your Highness. Quick, climb into this barrel!"

The king jumped in, not realizing that it was half full of molasses. When he was covered with the sticky goo, Nanda cried, "No, you can't hide there, he will see you. Quick, get into this sack!"

The king leaped out of the barrel and into the large sack. It was half full of cotton and feathers, which stuck to the molasses. The king was covered from head to foot, and looked strange indeed.

"No!" cried Nanda. "That won't do either. He will easily find you in the sack. You must run for it!"

The king climbed out of the sack and ran into the yard. The prime minister was waiting and yelled, "The Bosung Pohoo! I have captured the Bosung Pohoo!" Waving his sword in the air, he chased the king all the way back to the palace.

The villagers gathered in the streets and cheered as the ugly, fluffy-feathered creature ran past. How happy they were to find that the Bosung Pohoo was just a silly beast after all, and nothing to be frightened of.

At last the king reached the safety of his palace. The prime minister followed right behind.

"Trusted minister," panted the embarrassed king, "please forgive me. I was wrong. I promise never to trouble you or Nanda again if you will promise never to tell the people that I was the Bosung Pohoo."

The prime minister agreed, and he and his clever Nanda lived very happily together for many long years.

LITTLE JACK & LAZY JOHN

A Tale From France

TWIN BROTHERS ONCE owned a bakery. They were named Little Jack and Lazy John, and looked so much alike that it was difficult to tell one from the other. The only real difference between them was that Little Jack was industrious and hard-working while Lazy John was quite lazy.

Little Jack was also a happy lad, without a care in the world. He sang as he worked and he chuckled as he rested, and never was he seen to wear a frown. Lazy John, on the other hand, was as clever as he was lazy.

One day the king stopped at the bakery and asked for a fresh loaf of bread. Little Jack served him with great joy and smiled, sang, and laughed as he took a hot loaf from the oven and wrapped it in brown paper.

"Are you always this happy?" asked the king.

"Oh yes, Sire!" laughed Little Jack. "I've never known a sad day in my entire life."

The king looked stern and said, "Everyone has troubles. It's a rule of life. And it's up to me to see that you are not an exception to this rule. I will ask you three difficult questions. If you haven't answered them by noon tomorrow, your bakery will be burned to the ground."

Little Jack looked worried and his voice shook as he asked, "What are the questions, Your Majesty?"

"First, how much am I worth? Second, how much does the moon weigh? And third, what am I thinking? You have until noon tomorrow."

The king rode away. For the first time since he was a babe, Little Jack began to cry. Lazy John came in and asked what in the world the trouble could be. Little Jack explained and now his brother began to laugh.

"Let me go to the palace and answer the questions for you," said Lazy John. "I'm sure that I can save our bakery."

When the sun reached its highest peak the following day, Lazy John entered the palace with a smile spread across his face.

"Have you answers to my questions?" asked the king.

"Yes, Sire," said Lazy John. "Good answers, each one."

"Excellent," replied the king. "Remember what will happen if you fail. Let's begin. First, you must tell me how much I am worth."

"Twenty-nine pieces of silver," said the twin. "Our Lord was sold for thirty pieces and you are worth one less."

"A good answer," conceded the king. "Now tell me how much the moon weighs."

"It weighs one pound, Your Worship."

"One pound? Why only one pound?" demanded the king.

"Because, Sire, it has four quarters, and four quarter-pounds make one whole pound."

"Very well," said the king. "You are twice right. But in order to save your bakery, you must tell me what I'm thinking."

"That is easiest of all, my King. You are thinking that I'm Little Jack, the baker, but you are wrong. I'm his brother, Lazy John!"

The king realized that he had been tricked by the cleverest of men and began to laugh. He gave Lazy John a handsome reward and sent him home. The twin brothers kept their bakery for many long and happy years.

THE COLOSSAL PUMPKIN

A Tale From Africa

LONG AGO IN a West African village, a pumpkin grew so large that the villagers called it Feegba. Feegba was a good name, as it means "big thing." Never before in the history of the village had a pumpkin grown so large! It sat on the ground but stood as tall as a man or a woman. It was as round as a small house, and as orange as the bright sun. It was the most magnificent pumpkin ever to grow in all of Africa!

One day a farmer and his son decided that the pumpkin was ready to harvest. They brought their largest knife to the field and began to cut it open.

"Ouch!" cried the pumpkin. "That hurts. Take your knife away."

"No," responded the farmer. "We are going to make you into soup for the entire village. A feast is being held in your honor this very night, and we must prepare you for the main course."

"Eating me is not the way to honor me. Take your knife and leave me alone!"

"You are ripe," explained the farmer. "We must eat you before you spoil." And he sliced through the stem with his sharp knife.

"Now I'm angry!" said the pumpkin. "And you must be taught a lesson."

Very slowly at first, the pumpkin began to roll toward the farmer and his son. It was on a downhill slope and soon began to gather speed.

The farmer dropped his knife and yelled, "Run, boy, run!" Away they fled, running toward the village below.

Faster and faster, the colossal pumpkin rolled after them. Soon the father and son were running headlong down the hillside, stumbling over rocks and dodging trees in their flight. The pumpkin was right behind, and gaining on them with each roll. It squashed an abandoned hut and flattened a clump of trees. Then it smashed into a small hill and rolled it down flat!

The man and his son were exhausted and couldn't run much further. Still the pumpkin flew down the mountainside, getting closer and closer. At last, father and son came to a huge, jagged rock and fell down behind it in a heap. The pumpkin couldn't slow down, and it hit the rock with a mighty blow! It split down the middle into two gigantic halves....

This is the part of the story that is difficult to believe. Most people think it is simply nonsense and couldn't have really happened. But you and I know that anything can happen in a story—and sometimes, the stranger the better! This is what happened:

The bottom half of the pumpkin became the earth.

The top half became the sky.

The seeds became all the bright stars.

And, for as long as they lived, neither the farmer nor his son ever cut open a pumpkin again.

GRANDDAUGHTER'S SLED

A Tale From Russia

A MAN NAMED Ivan lived with his elderly father and young daughter. At that time, so long ago, old people were thought to be useless. They were taken to the forest and left to die, all alone. Now that the old man was feeble and could no longer earn a living, Ivan tied him onto his daughter's sled.

"Where are you taking Grandfather?" asked the girl.

"To the forest," replied Ivan.

"But why, Father? He is too weak to cut down trees or pick berries."

"Never mind why, Daughter. It's something I must do."

"Can I come too?" asked the girl.

"Yes, but ask no more questions."

The girl ran behind the sled, stopping here and there to pick wildflowers for her grandfather. When they came to the middle of the forest, Ivan said, "I'm sorry to leave you here, Father, but you know how it is among our people."

"You can't leave Grandfather out here," said the girl. "He will starve or be killed by the wolves."

"He is old and can no longer work. I have no choice, Daughter."

The girl thought for a moment and said, "But we can't leave my sled behind, because when you grow old, I'll need it to carry you into the forest."

Ivan frowned and then realized the truth of the girl's statement. "You are right, Daughter. Let's take Grandfather home. But don't tell any of our neighbors that he is still with us."

They hid the old man in a back room and kept his existence a great secret.

Soon afterward, a terrible famine swept the land. Food became scarce and the people grew hungry. Ivan had less and less to take to his aged father. The old man did not complain.

The famine continued and the villagers ate the last of the wheat and rye. They even ate the seed grain and had nothing to plant in the spring. There was no hope of survival.

Ivan took his old father a small piece of hard bread and told him that the people were starving.

"Nonsense," said Grandfather. "Take the straw roof from the barn and thrash it well. You will find that there is more than a handful of grain left in the thatch. Plant the grain and you will get a healthy crop."

Ivan did as he was told and soon had a fine crop of rye. The villagers were grateful and asked him where he got such excellent advice.

"From my father, a wise man indeed."

"Your father is dead," said one of the villagers.

"Grandfather is *not* dead," explained Ivan's daughter. We have hidden him, but not his wisdom. Grandfather has saved *all* of our lives!"

So Grandfather came out of hiding, and from that time forth, old people were honored and respected in that village.

JUAN'S MAGUEY PLANT

A Tale From Mexico

JUAN LIVED IN the country and was quite poor. His only wealth was a huge maguey plant. Pronounced "*MAG-way*," Mexicans use it to make a fermented drink called *pulque*. It is also used to make a liquor called *tequila*. The plant can grow to be nine feet long and twenty feet tall!

Juan's maguey plant was the largest in all of Mexico, and he took great care of it. Using a gourd, he dipped the honey-water from its center and sold it to his many customers. Juan loved the plant and was often heard to say that it made the sweetest juice in the world.

Coyote heard of this boast and decided to have a taste. Late one night, he sneaked into Juan's yard and drank from the center of the plant. He sipped a mouthful of the honey-water and couldn't believe how delicious it was! He slurped up more and rolled his eyes in delight! Coyote couldn't help himself and drank all the juice, and then escaped into the darkness.

Juan saw Coyote's footprints the following morning. "Coyote must be stopped," he said, "or he will return each night to drink from my plant."

Using a long knife called a machete, Juan cut tall poles for a fence. He sharpened the poles on one end and drove them into the ground all around the maguey plant. Then he cut a small opening in the circle-fence, close to the ground. Clever Coyote would just fit through this door.

Juan climbed to the rooftop of his little house and waited for nightfall. A half-moon rose in the sky giving him enough light to see the thief trotting with an air of confidence into the yard. Coyote sniffed at the new fence and circled it three times before he spied the small doorway. He quickly slipped inside.

Juan quietly climbed down to the ground, picked up a heavy club and crept towards the plant. He could hear Coyote's greedy gulps coming from inside the fence.

"Now I've got you," said Juan to himself. "You'll never drink from my maguey plant again!" He smashed the side of the fence with his club and yelled at the top of his lungs, "TONIGHT, COYOTE, YOU DIE!"

Coyote jumped straight up into the air. Higher than the fence he jumped! But he fell right back down, inside the fence, and began to run in circles. He ran around and around, faster and faster, and kept missing the little doorway, he was traveling so fast!

Juan started to laugh. Never before had he seen anything so funny! He laughed harder and harder. He dropped the club and fell to the ground and giggled and chuckled and howled. He laughed so hard that his eyes began to water and he couldn't see what was happening.

Coyote slowed down his running in circles and finally found the door. He stuck his nose outside, then his entire head. Juan wiped his blurry eyes and found his club. He raised it high above his head and tried to bring it down. But he couldn't. He stood paralyzed with laughter as Coyote squeezed on out of the hole and ran away faster than ever before.

Juan laughed for another five minutes before he could finally stop and lower the club. "What a fright I gave him!" Juan said, still chuckling. "He'll never come back! Now I can sleep in peace."

That was true. Coyote had been frightened, and forever after, he stayed away from Juan's maguey plant.

THE DEVIL'S LUCK

A Tale From Hungary

LONG, LONG AGO, there lived a young peasant who decided to go forth into the wide world to seek both bride and fortune. After walking for several days, he came to a long, narrow bridge made of gleaming silver. He began to walk across it, but before he took two steps an old man with a long beard appeared from thin air and said, "Take your boots off and walk lightly upon this bridge, boy. It's the Devil's Bridge, and if he hears you coming, he will take you to the underworld." So saying, the old man vanished from sight.

The peasant pulled off his boots and walked slowly and quietly over the silver expanse. When he had reached the other end, the devil leapt up from under the bridge!

"Heard you coming, boy," said the devil with a grin. "Oh, you were trying hard to be quiet, and it's lucky for you that you did. I'm not even mad. I know that you seek a wife and I'm going to help you find a good one. Walk past the first six villages on this road and don't stop until you come to the seventh. In the seventh village, go to the seventh house. There you will find a man with seven daughters. Ask the youngest to be your bride. If she says yes, come back with her across this bridge, and I'll give you a proper wedding gift."

The youth agreed and, with a stout heart, began the journey to the seventh village. At the seventh house he found the man with seven daughters. The youngest was both intelligent and pretty, and, deciding that she could love him, she accepted the youth's proposal of marriage. Her father sent for the priest, and when the wedding feast had ended, the young couple set off for the silver bridge.

"This is the Devil's Bridge," explained the peasant to his bride. "We must take off our boots and walk lightly upon it."

They did so, but halfway across, the devil leapt up from underneath. "Heard you coming, friends," he said with a grin. "And the seven fat pigs at the end of the bridge are your wedding gift. Of course, in seven weeks' time I'll come to your door and ask seven questions. If you answer them correctly, you'll have seven years' good luck. If, however, you're wrong, seven years of suffering will follow."

The newlyweds drove the pigs home and set up housekeeping. The seven weeks flew by and the young man grew quite worried.

"Don't fret, dear husband," said the wife. "I'll answer the old devil's questions."

It was midnight on the seventh day of the seventh week that the devil came knocking at their door. "Are you ready to answer my seven questions?" said he.

"Yes," replied the bride.

"First, what is it that the world has only ONE of?"

"One sun in the heavens," came her answer.

"What about two?" asked the devil. "What is the most important thing that people have TWO of?"

"Two eyes to see everything under the sun."

"And three, what does THREE make?"

"A husband, wife, and child make three, and that makes a family."

"Yes," the devil continued, "but what do you say about FOUR?"

"A wagon must have four wheels in order to roll."

"And five?" he asked, "how about FIVE?"

"Four fingers and a thumb make five, and that's what it takes to hold a hammer to build or a sword to destroy."

"Six is next. What's your answer to SIX?"

"If you have but six hens, do not ask for a dozen eggs," said the woman.

"And finally, SEVEN," said the devil, "what say you to the last question?"

"A young couple with seven fat pigs need not beg from any other."

The devil smiled and said, "You have wisdom beyond your years, young lady. Your seven answers are correct." Then, he vanished.

Indeed, the peasant and his clever wife enjoyed good fortune for the next seven years, and far beyond. They even had seven blessed children of their own!

THE OFFICER OF HEAVEN

A Tale From China

ONE DAY TIGER walked through the jungle in search of his dinner. It wasn't long before he met Fox, and even though Fox looked thin and tough, Tiger decided to eat him.

"Prepare to die, little Fox, for I rule the jungle and I am hungry."

Fox was clever and said, "You are joking, Brother Tiger. You can't eat me. I'm too important."

"What do you mean, *important*?" demanded the hungry tiger.

"I'm an officer of Heaven. I've been appointed to watch over all the animals. That includes you as well, Brother Tiger."

"*You*, watch over me?" growled Tiger. "Why would *you* have to watch over me?"

"To keep the evil spirits away. Heaven has given me special powers to keep all the jungle animals safe."

"How do I know that you are telling the truth?" asked the skeptical tiger. "You may be playing a trick just to save your skinny bones."

"If you want a demonstration of my power, we have merely to walk through the jungle," said Fox.

"Very well," said Tiger, "but you must walk in front of me so that I can keep my eyes on you. I know how tricky you can be."

"As you wish," said Fox with a sly grin, "just as you wish."

Through the jungle they walked, little Fox in front and big Tiger close behind. They soon came upon a small herd of deer. The deer ignored Fox, but they moment they saw Tiger, they leaped into the air and fled for their lives!

"Hmmm," thought Tiger, "it requires power to make an entire herd run. Perhaps Fox truly is an officer of Heaven."

Just then they met Water Buffalo, one of the largest of the jungle animals. Realizing that Tiger was near, she turned and ran, leaving a trail of broken trees and vines.

"Yes," thought the tiger, "an officer of Heaven deserves respect."

They continued along the trail for a short while longer and saw Elephant. Elephant saw Fox and completely ignored him.

"So!" snarled Tiger, "Elephant does not fear you, Little Fox!"

Upon hearing Tiger's angry growl, Elephant began to panic! He raised his trunk high in the air, trumpeted loudly, and ran away, trampling the ground as he went.

For the first time in his life, Tiger grew afraid and said, "It is just as you have said all along, my friend. Truly you are an officer of Heaven and have the power to keep the evil spirits away. Never would I eat one so important."

"Heaven is pleased with your wise decision, friend Tiger," said Fox. Under his breath he muttered, "And so am I."

THE KING WHO BELIEVED EVERYTHING

A Tale From Austria

THERE ONCE WAS a king who believed everything. If one of his advisors said the castle was floating in the air, he believed it. If his wife, the queen, explained that she was invited to a tea party at the bottom of the sea, he believed it. If the royal gardener claimed that his beautiful roses grew from seed to blossom in one day, the king believed that as well.

To tell the truth, the king didn't *want* to believe everything. Thus he promised a chest of gold and the title of "Highest Advisor to the Court" to anyone who could tell him something that he wouldn't believe. To those who tried and failed, he promised a year's stay in the dungeon.

People formed a long line at the castle door, each hoping to win the prize. To each outlandish tale he heard, the king said, "Yes, I believe that. Off to the dungeon with you!"

A year and a day went by and the king was growing quite discouraged. Not once had he been able to say, "No, that is false. I do *not* believe it!" Thus he added a second chest of gold to the reward.

An old farmer named Wilhelm heard of the king's generous offer and decided to visit him. "O mighty King, I will tell you about my last great adventure and you will not believe it."

"Very well," replied the king, "but if you fail..."

"Yes, of course," said Wilhelm, "but let me tell you my story. I planted beans in my garden last week, and one of the stalks grew one hundred feet tall!"

"I believe you," said the king.

"I climbed up the stalk, and by the time I got to the top, it had grown two hundred feet tall!"

"I believe you," said the king.

"The stalk kept growing at an alarming rate and I soon found myself in the clouds. A roadway appeared and I leaped from the stalk and landed in the middle of it."

"I still believe you," said the king.

"I walked down the road for a few miles and came to a large golden bird. The bird could speak and told me to climb upon her back. I did so and she rose into the air, carrying me to heaven."

"Go on," said the king, "I believe every word."

"It was a wonderful visit!" explained Wilhelm. "Angels filled the sky with wondrous beauty. I also saw several of my dear, departed friends, and they seemed so happy. Then I saw my old parents, and they looked young and healthy. They wore royal robes and golden crowns. My heart was filled with joy!"

"Yes, I believe you," said the king.

"But then, O wise King, I saw *your* parents. I remembered them from the time I was a boy. And I fear I bring sad news. They did not look happy or healthy. They were thin and dressed in rags, and were begging for money."

"NO!" cried the king. "That is false! You did not see them! I do NOT BELIEVE YOU!"

So it was that a clever farmer named Wilhelm became rich and earned the title of "Highest Advisor to the Court."

HUNGRY SPIDER

A Tale From Africa (Ashanti Tribe)

SPIDER WAS HUNGRY! He was always hungry. Spider was greedy as well. All the animals knew that, when it was mealtime, Spider had many tricks, and for Spider, it was *always* mealtime.

One day Turtle left his home in the pond and went on a long journey. He traveled slowly through the jungle and finally arrived at Spider's house. They had never met each other before this, and Spider reluctantly invited Turtle to stay for dinner. Spider liked to talk to strangers, as they had interesting stories to tell. But he hated to feed them because they ate food that he wanted for himself.

"Friend Turtle," said Spider, "you must be tired after your long trip. Go down to the river and refresh yourself. I'll prepare our dinner while you are gone."

"How kind of you," said Turtle. "I'll hurry as I'm quite hungry." Turtle followed the trail to the water's edge and scrambled in. It was good to cool down and feel clean again. He crawled out of the river and hurried back to Spider's house. Delicious odors filled the air. It was time to eat!

Turtle walked in and saw the food on the table. "Thank you for inviting me to stay for dinner, Spider," said Turtle. "I haven't eaten all day."

"You are most welcome, Turtle," said Spider with a frown. "But in this part of the country, we don't sit at the table with muddy feet."

Turtle looked at his feet. Indeed, they were muddy. His feet were wet from the river and the trail was thick with dust. He was most embarrassed. He excused himself and walked all the way back to the river to wash them off. He dried them carefully on the grass and hurried back to Spider. But he was too late. Spider had eaten all the food. Turtle was disappointed, but too polite to

complain. He slept hungry that night and left for home in the morning even hungrier!

Several months later, Spider went on a long journey. He arrived at Turtle's house and asked if he could spend the night.

"Of course, friend Spider," said Turtle. "I remember how good you were to me."

"I'm famished!" exclaimed Spider. "Could we eat right away?"

"I'll dive to the bottom of the pond and prepare a feast," said Turtle. "Wait here and I'll call you when all is ready." Turtle gathered his best-tasting food, and set it on a long table at the bottom of the pond. Then he swam to the surface and said, "Please join me, Spider. Dinner is served."

Spider leaped into the water and tried to dive down. But he weighed so little that he couldn't stay under water, let alone sink to the bottom. Turtle had already started to eat, so Spider kicked and jerked and splashed with all of his strength. And he stayed right on top.

Turtle swam to the surface and said, "Friend Spider, come down and enjoy the meal. It's quite good, if I do say so."

Spider had an idea! He scrambled back to shore and picked up several heavy pebbles. He stuffed them in his coat pockets to weigh him down. Spider then hopped back into the pond and sank quickly to the bottom. The food was half gone, but what was left looked delicious! He had started to take a big bite when Turtle said, "Friend Spider, in this part of the jungle, it's considered bad manners to eat with your coat on."

Spider didn't want to be impolite. So he slipped out of his coat and reached for another morsel of food. But before he could grab hold of it, he bobbed to the surface like a cork! Spider cried as he floated about, watching Turtle down on the bottom of the pond eating the rest of the food.

It is said that one kindness deserves another.

THE FIRST LESSON

A Tale From Brazil

A MIGHTY HUNTER named Gahan fell in love with a beautiful young woman named Mirra. When he asked her to marry him, she said, "You are a good-looking man, Gahan, and a skilled warrior. But you lack wisdom. I cannot marry a man who isn't wise."

"Then I shall learn wisdom!" declared Gahan.

The old chieftain of the neighboring tribe was called Tierno, and he was said to be wise. Gahan paddled his canoe down the river to learn from him. When he arrived, the village children showed him the dwelling place of Tierno.

"I have come to learn wisdom," explained the warrior.

"To get it, you must want it more than anything else in the world," said the chieftain.

"Yes," said Gahan, "more than anything else, that is what I want."

"Then I shall give you the first lesson. Come with me."

Tierno led Gahan down to the river and told him to kneel down in the shallow water. He did so and the old man pushed Gahan's head underwater and held it there until the youth was half drowned! At last, Tierno let go of his stronghold, and Gahan came up sputtering and coughing.

"Tell me what you were thinking of there with your head underwater," demanded the old man.

"Air to breathe!" cried Gahan.

"Are you sure? Did you think instead of how brave you are, or how skilled a hunter?"

"No," said Gahan, "I thought only of air."

"This is the first lesson. When you want wisdom as much as you wanted air, you will become a wise man."

Gahan returned to his village and met with Mirra.

"Did Tierno teach you how to be wise?" she asked.

Gahan lowered his head and spoke softly. "No, my beautiful Mirra. He taught me that air is more important than wisdom."

"In that case," she said, "I will marry you."

Gahan couldn't believe what he had heard! "But it will take me many years before I am wise. I'll be old and have weakness in my eyes and legs."

"I know," said Mirra with a smile. "But you have shown me that you now have two qualities that I value as much as wisdom—honesty and humility. So now you have taken the first step to finding wisdom and I am satisfied."

PEDER & THE WATER SPRITE

A Tale From Sweden

ONCE LONG AGO, an old man called his son, whose name was Peder, to his bedside. "I'm soon going to die," he said, "and I'm sorry that I have nothing more to leave you than a coil of rope. It's a good rope, and I'm sure that you will find a way to prosper with it."

Peder's father died the following day. After the burial service, the lad wiped away his tears and carried the coil of rope into the forest. Soon he had an idea and used the rope to make a snare. It wasn't long before he caught a young squirrel, and, soon after, a frisky rabbit. He placed both in a wicker basket and, carrying the basket with him, went in search of larger game.

Peder knew that an old bear liked to take long naps in a cave near the shore of a large lake. The boy sat on a rock and dangled his feet in the cold water as he began to make a snare large enough to catch a bear! Just then an ugly and very dangerous water sprite swam up from the bottom of the lake and said, "Why are your stinky feet in my water?"

"I'm making the largest snare in Sweden," said Peder, "and I'm going to catch all the sprites who try to escape from the lake."

The sprite scowled and said, "Shame on you, boy, for even thinking that you could catch me. I'm much too fast for the likes of you. In fact, I challenge you to a race to the top of that tree over there."

"Oh, I don't have time for a silly race right now," explained Peder, "so I'll let my little cousin run for me."

The lad released the squirrel from the basket. It ran to the tree and was sitting on the highest branch before the sprite could blink three times!

"Your cousin is a quick climber," admitted the sprite, "but I know that I could beat you in a race across the ground."

"I'm too busy with this snare," said Peder, as he kept knotting the rope. "I'll let you race against my little brother."

Peder released the rabbit from the basket. It laid back its long ears and sped across the rocky shore and into the forest undergrowth before the sprite could twice blink his eyes!

"Your little brother is a fast runner," said the sprite, "but still, I am strong, much stronger than you realize. I challenge you to a wrestling match."

"I'll never get this snare made if I take time to play your games," said Peder. "If you want to wrestle, go up to the cave and wake up my old grandfather. He will be happy to meet your challenge."

The water sprite ran to the cave and yanked on the sleeping bear's whiskers while shouting, "Wake up, old man! Your grandson said that you would wrestle with me!"

An angry roar shook the mountainside as the bear awoke and lumbered out of the dark cave. Then he stood on his hind legs with his massive paws held high, ready to do battle.

The sprite blinked once and ran back to the water's edge. "Your grandfather is strong, that I admit," he said. Then, after hesitating a moment, the sprite asked, "What do you want, to leave me and all the other water sprites alone?"

Peder thought for a moment and said, "Enough gold coins to fill my hat."

"Agreed," said the sprite, and he dove to the bottom of the deep lake.

Meanwhile, Peder cut a hole in the top of his hat and scooped out a pit in the ground. Then he placed the hat upside down, over the pit. When the sprite returned, he poured the coins into the hat, which, of course, simply fell through the hole and into the pit.

"That's an awfully big hat," grumbled the sprite. "I'll have to dive again for more coins."

He returned the second time with enough gold to fill both pit and hat, and Peder was pleased. "Thank you, sprite," said Peder. "Now you and your friends are safe. And any time you feel like another race or wrestling match, just let me know."

"No, thank you," said the sprite. "If you are anything like the rest of your family, I'll just stay home at the bottom of the lake." With that the sprite turned and quickly dove back down into the cold water.

THE GOAT & THE ROCK

A Tale From Tibet

IT HAPPENED ONE day that a milk-seller was busily doing business. He walked up and down the winding, narrow streets of town carrying a large clay jug filled with milk and calling in his loudest voice, "Milk for sale! Fresh milk for sale!" Whenever someone needed milk, they would open their door to him. The peddler would pour his milk into the customer's pitcher, collect a few coins and continue on his way, crying, "Fresh milk for sale!"

Soon it was lunchtime and the peddler decided to rest in the shade of a large rock. He set the heavy milk jug, now half-empty, down on a flat spot on top of the rock and began to eat his hard cheese and dark bread.

Soon a goatherd came down the road driving a small number of bleating animals in front of him. Upon seeing the milk-seller, he called out a loud and happy, "Hello!" The sudden sound startled the lead goat and she leaped up onto the rock and knocked the jug over. It fell to the ground and broke into several pieces.

The milk-seller was furious and demanded payment for both jug and lost milk, but the herdsman explained that it wasn't his fault, it was the fault of the goat. They argued long into the afternoon and at last agreed to take their case before the local judge.

The judge listened patiently to each of the men and then said, "It's obvious that the milk-seller has lost his jug and his milk through no fault of his own. Without his jug, he will not be able to conduct his business and feed his family.

"It's just as obvious that the goatherd is not at fault. He meant no harm with his friendly greeting. If he sold his goats to pay for the damage, he would not be able to feed his family.

"Therefore, the blame lies with the goat and the rock. I'll have them arrested at once. They shall be tried at noon tomorrow."

The goat and rock were placed under arrest and taken to prison. The goat went peacefully, but the rock was stubborn and had to be carried by twenty strong men.

News of the strange event traveled swiftly throughout the city and everyone wanted to attend the trial of the goat and the rock. The people knew that the judge was fair, but this sounded like madness! The following day, the courtyard was packed with curious citizens.

The judge smiled when he saw the crowd and ordered the guards to close the gates and lock everyone in. Then he spoke to the assembled citizens:

"You have all come to witness the trial of a goat and rock. But, as you must realize, we have no laws by which to judge them. Therefore, you must think that I've gone mad, and you've actually come to see me do something foolish.

"I'm disappointed in you for thinking such a terrible thing about me, and I've decided to fine each of you one penny for 'improper thoughts.' You must pay the fine to leave the courtyard."

The people laughed and happily paid the small fine. Of course, the judge gave all the pennies to the milk-seller, who was then able to buy another jug, fill it with fresh milk, and continue on down the winding streets, joyfully calling, "Milk for sale! Fresh milk for sale!"

Notes

Motifs given (where appropriate) are from Margaret Read MacDonald, *The Storyteller's Sourcebook: A Subject, Title, and Motif Index to Folklore Collections for Children.* (Detroit: Gale/Neal-Schuman, 1982).

Old Joe & the Carpenter
United States   **Page 13**

I first heard the bare bones of this, my signature story, from an elementary school librarian in Bellingham, Washington, in 1977. I simplified the plot and strengthened the ending during many years of telling it aloud. Perhaps the first recorded version is found in *North Carolina Folklore,* "A Job of Work," by Manly Wade Wellman, Volume III, No. 1, July, 1955. The story was told to Mr. Wellman in 1951 by an old bee hunter named Green who lived near Bat Cave in Henderson County, North Carolina.

The Tug of War
Africa   **Page 15**

K22.0.4. An excellent tale for young children in need of an ego boost. Another version of this tale is found in *The Merry Little Fox and Other Animal Stories* by Norah Montgomerie (New York: Abclard-Schuman, 1964), pp. 28-31.

The Listening Cap
Japan   **Page 19**

D1067.2.1. After sharing this tale, I'm often asked if such caps really exist, and where one can be found. For another telling, see *The Magic Listening Cap: More Folk Tales From Japan* by Yoshiko Uchida (New York: Harcourt, Brace, 1955), pp. 2-10.

Rabbit's Last Race
Mexico   **Page 21**

K11.1. One of many variants of the "race" won by using the relatives to deceive the braggart. Usually it's hare vs. turtle. I've heard another about a family of ants deceiving an elephant. A good source (terrapin defeats hare) is Joel Chandler Harris's *The Favorite Uncle Remus* (Boston: Houghton Mifflin, 1948), pp. 86-90.

Alexander, the Dwarf & the Troll
Denmark   **Page 25**

H321.1. The troll wife is a delight to portray. A great opportunity for big-time expression! Another telling is found in *A Book of Ogres and Trolls* by Ruth Manning-Sanders (New York: Dutton, 1972), pp. 123-127.

Medicine Wolf
Native American   **Page 29**

Legends of the Blackfoot Nation were recorded from oral history near the end of the nineteenth century. This story unfolds so simply, it nearly tells itself. See *Myths of the North American Indians* by Lewis Spence (London: George G. Harrap, 1914).

Señor Rattlesnake Learns to Fly
Mexico   **Page 31**

A similar motif to the African variant in which tortoise does the flying, talking, and falling. See *African Village Folktales* by Edna Mason Kaula (New York: World, 1968), pp. 80-83.

Grandfather Spider's Feast
Africa   **Page 35**

J2183.1.3. A great story for the classroom. Play narrator and have the children enact the plot. Another version of this tale is found in *The Hat-Shaking Dance, and Other Tales From The Gold Coast* by Harold Courlander and Albert Kofi Prempeh (New York: Harcourt, Brace, 1957) pp. 18-19.

The Mirror
Korea   **Page 39**

J1795.2. Hold up the (imaginary) mirror and make *all* the appropriate faces when sharing this story. It's fun! See *The Story Bag: A Collection of Korean Folk Tales* by So-Un Kim (Rutland, Vermont: Tuttle, 1955) pp. 44-50.

Damon & Pythias
Ancient Greece   **Page 43**

Build the suspense slowly in the telling. Make the pregnant pause between the falling of the ax and the arrival of Pythias a breath-holder. Another source is found in *Favorite Folktales and Fables* by Joanna Strong (New York: Hart, 1950), pp. 67-71.

The Princess Who Could Not Cry
Original   **Page 47**

While conducting a Young Author workshop at an elementary school, I asked the children how they would try to make her cry without hurting her. Their ideas are included in this story.

The Lion's Whisker
Africa   **Page 51**

B848.21. Several variations upon this theme exist in African folk-literature. I've found this one to be an excellent story for weddings and anniversary celebrations. See *African Village Folktales* by Edna Mason Kaula (New York: World, 1968), pp. 142-145.

How the Mosquitoes Left Kambara
Fiji   **Page 53**

A2434.2.4. While telling at a summer camp, my young listeners and I were bothered by a hungry horde of pesky mosquitoes. Fortunately I remembered this tale. See also, *Tales From The South Pacific Islands* by Anne Gittens (Owings Mills, Maryland: Stemmer House, 1977) pp. 3-10.

Clever Gretel
Germany   **Page 57**

K2137. Older children like the cleverness and fun of this story. If you enjoy the telling, your listeners will laugh! Another version is found in *Grimm's Tales For Young and Old* by Ralph Manheim (New York: Doubleday, 1977), pp. 272-274.

Ah Shung Catches a Ghost
China   **Page 59**

A fun addition to a Halloween program, especially if the other selections are really scary! Create a whispery voice for the ghost. See also *Folk Tales of China* by Lee Wyndham (Indianapolis: Bobbs-Merrill, 1963), pp. 48-51.

Coyote Steals Spring
Native American   **Page 63**

I love the one-pointedness of this story. Coyote knows what he wants and how to get it. Tell it on cold, wintry days. A variant of this Northwest tale is found in *The Talking Stone: An Anthology of Native American Tales and Legends* by Dorothy DeWitt (New York: Greenwillow, 1979), pp. 113-117.

The Chirimía
Guatemala   **Page 65**

This tale, which explains the origin of the chirimía, is popular in Guatemala. A more complete version is found in *The King of The Mountains, A Treasury of Latin American Folk Stories* by M. A. Jagendorf and R.S. Boggs (New York: Vanguard, 1960), pp. 132-135.

Natural Habits
Africa   **Page 69**

K263.1. One of my "natural habits" on stage is to take a complete breath (inhale-exhale) between the introduction and actual story. What's one of yours? Pantomime is encouraged for this story! See *More Favorite Stories*

Old and New For Boys and Girls by Sidonie M. Gruenberg (New York: Doubleday, 1948) pp. 105-108.

The Magic Pot
China   **Page 71**

D1652.5.7.1. After this tale I often hear, "Wow! I want one of those pots!" Materialism must be a timeless and multicultural trait. Another version is in *The Arbuthnot Anthology of Children's Literature* by May Hill Arbuthnot (Chicago: Scott Forsman, 1961), pp. 333-334.

Ada & the Rascals
Holland   **Page 75**

I love it when bad guys are outsmarted with genuine intelligence as opposed to luck. Another telling is found in *The Buried Treasure and Other Picture Tales* by Eulalie Steinmetz Ross (Philadelphia: Lippincott, 1958), pp. 127-134.

The Miser
United States   **Page 79**

J2478. An old story with a contemporary theme. Such is the power of the heart. I tell it to business groups working on improving the "bottom line." It's similar to a Jewish tale found in *More Wise Men of Helm* by Solomon Simon (New York: Behrmen House, 1965), pp. 77-78.

The Bosung Pohoo
India   **Page 83**

K1601. Another strong and intelligent woman from the folk traditions. More, please! See also, *The Fables of India* by Joseph Gaer (Boston: Little, Brown, 1955), pp. 18-20.

Little Jack & Lazy John
France   **Page 85**

H711.1. A popular plot with the king always asking, "How much am I worth?" Is it any wonder monarchies are essentially a thing of the past? I first heard this as a French peasant's story. A similar version is found in Norway. See *Norwegian Folk Tales* by Peter Christen Asbornsen (New York: Viking, 1960), pp. 15-16.

The Colossal Pumpkin
Africa   **Page 89**

A641.3. A delightful twist of plot! Note how the listening intensifies when you get to "This is the part of the story that is hard to believe...." I once heard a Hawaiian tell a similar tale about a gigantic calabash. This African version is also found in *Guillot's African Folk Tales* by Rene Guillot (New York: Franklin Watts, 1965), pp. 95-97.

Granddaughter's Sled
Russia   **Page 91**

J121.3. In the telling, I trust the story to balance innocence with hardship. My voice, gestures, and emotions follow accordingly. Try it. Another version is found in *More Tales of Faraway Folk* by Babette Deutsch and Avraham Yarmolinsky (New York: Harper & Row, 1963), pp. 63-68.

Juan's Maguey Plant
Mexico   **Page 95**

I place this story in the middle of a program and, when I *genuinely* laugh (as Juan), an amazing result occurs. My listeners are given the freedom to laugh back, and laugh they do! One of the original written versions is found in "The Little Animals of Mexico," contributed by Dan Storm to *Coyote Wisdom* (Texas Folk-Lore Society Publications, No. XIV, 1938). It is reprinted in *A Harvest of World Folktales* edited by Milton Rugoff (New York: Viking, 1949), pp. 595-598.

The Devil's Luck
Hungary   **Page 97**

A left-brain story! Students who excel in math and science seem to especially enjoy it. Ask them to come up with different answers to the seven questions. Another version is found in *13 Devils* by Dorothy Gladys Spicer (New York: Coward-McCann, 1967), pp. 25-32.

The Officer of Heaven
China   **Page 101**

J684.1.1. Sometimes it's Tiger, sometimes it's Lion, but it's always Fox who wins in the end. This is similar to a story found in *Favorite Children's Stories From China and Tibet* by Lotta Carswell Hume (Rutland, VT: Charles E. Tuttle, 1962), pp. 67-68.

The King Who Believed Everything
Austria   **Page 105**

H342.3. There exist several versions of this story, each with its own variety of tall tales used to force the king to say, "That's a lie!" In the classroom, ask the children to come up with their own sequence of lies. Select a king (or queen) and ask him/her to choose a winner. See *Tales From Atop A Russian Stove* by Higonnet-Schnopper (Chicago: Albert Whitman, 1973), pp. 21-29.

Hungry Spider
Africa   **Page 107**

    Spider, the trickster, usually comes out on top. It's fun as well as refreshing to see him outsmarted! Telling this story improves any gesture inhibitions one might have. Another version is found in *The Cow-Tail Switch and Other West African Stories* by Harold Courlander and George Herzog (New York: Holt, 1947), pp. 107-112.

The First Lesson
Brazil   **Page 111**

    An "integrated" tale: part folk and part fiction. I love the simple truths this story brings forth. It's effective with adult and business groups, as well as in schools. A junior-high student once asked me to send her boyfriend to the old chieftain, Tierno, as soon as possible!

Peder & the Water Sprite
Sweden   **Page 113**

    After sharing this story, an elderly Swede told me that a more accurate name for a water sprite is "Necken." See also, *Fairy Tales From Sweden* by Irma Kaplan (Chicago: Follett, 1967), pp. 200-208.

The Goat & the Rock
Tibet   **Page 117**

    J1141.3.4.1. In some stories, the rock is tried and lashed for stealing a child's money. This version is similar to a tale in *The Tiger's Whisker, and Other Tales and Legends From Asia and the Pacific* by Harold Courlander (New York: Harcourt, Brace, 1959), pp. 24-28.